IT'S ALL K.

PERCEPTION OF A SELF-LOATHING FOOL

AANYA ROY

Made with ♥ on the Notion Press Platform
www.notionpress.com

- To everyone who stuck around and to the ones who didn't -

Contents

Contents

Contents

Foreword

Manuscript's introduction from the people who have read it

Hi readers,

This book, *"It's All K"*, holds a special place in my heart as it is a collection of the author, my best friend's thoughts captured on paper in the form of beautiful, small poems. Some of you may find yourself relating deeply to certain pieces, while others might leave you feeling a bit puzzled, but by the end, you'll understand what this book is truly about. It's not here to give a "moral" or teach a "lesson"; it's simply her, sharing her recent life experiences, which I hope some of you will connect to and may find pieces of yourselves within her words.

For me, "K" has two meanings:- "okay" and "a treasured one." Lastly, always remember whatever you're going through, 'it will all be okay' in the end .

- **Prathana Khanna**

Coming from a person who has closely followed the authors journey, I can say this book is very authentic .To be honest when I read the book it felt like my thoughts were written on a piece of paper. It felt like the book knows you deeply, If you can't express how you feel, this is where you go.

-**Kripa mehra**

It's all okay when deep down we know it's not. This book doesn't represent just one person, but many others like me and you—those of us who are stuck here, not by mistake, obviously. We have so many friends, yet we can't share those things (the 3 a.m. thoughts) with anyone. Who knew that these thoughts could find their place in a book? But not just any book—an emotion in every line. And I'm not saying this just because my best friend is the writer, but because I can relate to each one of them. I think you can, too. We have to let go; we don't have a choice, do we? And trust me, you won't regret reading this one.

- **Kanishka Chaudhary**

This piece of literature holds the ache that comes when we're measured against others—a feeling all too familiar for many. They say comparison is the thief of joy, but to me, it's even more than that; it's a killer of joy, quietly eating away at self-worth and confidence. These pages aren't here to impress; they're here to express, to lay bare the insecurities and sadness that comparison brings. It's a voice for anyone who's ever felt small in someone else's shadow.

-Yat amias (context : Mom, but why only Sofia)

Preface

It is all about how you percieve. For me it's reality, all that i have seen and experienced.

***"It's all K."* can have different meanings for me and you** . It might be a person for me and might just be " it's all okay" for you and that is where i find what i have written . These free verses must be read and imagined in different perspectives.The book varies and connects the aspect of my life that i ponder about , which brings me to think and then to write.

I know that i haven't delivered the best in me but it comes from my soul anyways .The parts i was afraid to share but here i am . Topics that i ignored yet stayed in my subconcious Anyway. **Love , longing , hurt, hate and Life**. Everything that i have taken upon, all these years .Events i stopped and noticed.Being a 16 year old teenager who thinks she has seen enough in life to atleast be capable to share. This is a manuscript of how i view my surrounding . **I hope you find even a fraction of what i found in this in some way or the other .**

-Aanya Roy

Acknowledgements

To be honest, i'd like to thank *me*. To make it till here . Young Aanya would have been proud.

My mother has played a huge part in motivating me thorough this alongside my friends .

Last but definetly not the least, as you will read i'd like to thank the person who triggered the writing in me

even if he/she isn't a part of my life anymore.

Thankyou .

Prologue

PLAYLIST

Not a narrative , just a perspective

Margaret -(feat. Bleachers) and Lana Del Rey

The 1 - Taylor Swift

Love Yourself - Justin Bieber

Dreamer - Spencer Arjang

In My Room - Chance Peña

Slipping Through My fingers - ABBA

I love you so - The Walters

Hey Jude - The beatles

Beautiful Boy - John Lenon

misses- Dominic Fike

You're so Vain - Carly Simson

Lovefool- The Cardigans

1. Always Almost

We were always 'almost'
You and i, repeatedly
Circle back to what is written for us
To always being 'almost'.
We were never nothing
Not friends
never something .
Just as we figured that
We will always be almost
"Never something and never nothing"
Now ,'we' or 'us' doesn't exist .
We aren't even almost
But the memories of it
Alas!.
Will be the most of my being.

2. Sweet coffee latte

I was easy
Not to get , to be liked
I act as you wish
Will make you addicted
to a *sweet coffee latte.*
So when i get bitter, by fault-
Be the coffee, in its real taste
in its real state.
You'll complain like never before.

You'll show me the way out, throw me away.
Replace me with a sweeter one .
You only seem to like the perfect amount,
Not all of it at once.
There's no compromise,
The coffee for it being *coffee.*
Will be hated like never before.

3. Mom, but why only Sofia ?

(I'm pretty sure we all have a "**Sofia** " in our lives . The prettier and the more liked one. No matter how hard you try you fail to match their charm. What if i tell you it isn't you but people who fail to see more than the beauty that lies in their glances , which in the end will mean nothing . Never let "Sofia " take away your efforts , like i did. It can be anyone in your life . It's a friend in my life whom i love. Maybe it's someone else in yours . Whosover it may be , never lose your self trying to shine against their glitter . Who knows? you aren't meant for the short-termed glittery shimmer or just for the eye -liking. Maybe you are gold , meant for eternal allure .)

Mom why is it
That Sofia is considered beautiful but not me?
I love her , she is my bestfriend.
She is the kind of pretty that everybody likes.
Perfectly curled hair,
The perfect way to just exist and be seen.
Mom, i should just stop eating.
Maybe , then i'd stand a chance?
Mom, you said i'm the prettiest
But, why is that i don't get what I wanted the most and Sofia gets it
just because she has that magazine model like face?

Mother why is that
The makeup she wears just is the perfect amount for her
And when i try, it looks like i'm trying too hard…?
Mom , on a serious note
Why is that the person i loved
My best-friend, day and night
Always asked about Sofia more?
The last time i checked , I was the one who
was there at his worst.
Just "being pretty" overlooks my companionship too?
Is that how the world works?
So inimical,so hostile-
Don't get me wrong mother
Even i consider her charismatic
But oh,
How i hate when it openly degrades my existence all at once .
But mother, how is so
that even you like Sofia better than me?
and even father finds her more appealing.
However, i do better at school,
but that doesn't compare to her appeal does it?
Even at my own house.

Oh, I see how the world works.
"being pretty" overlooks all that i have to offer.
I stand there,
to be valued

to be loved just as much,

Tried so hard to be considered just as liked.-

Why is it though, why don't i deserve ?

I am better at everything else,

i still fail to compare,

to her external features

Those perfectly shaded pink lips,

The admired feminine aura.

No matter how better or how talented of a person i become

All my life being a people pleaser has got me nothing but losing to bare minimum,

And a whole lot of "pretty".

Mother,

Sofia will be still be preferred.

I stopped trying to shine against her .

4. October.

• 8 •

It is not like other months.
As it arrives after whatever the hell September was,
It brings a whole new season .
Images of shedding leaves , tore hearts-
Woven with new characters entering my life in this very month,
cyclic every year.

A known feeling every year ,nostalgia
Every year October brings the plot twist which changes the way i operate,
the trajectory
Until next year ,the same month .

It comes in the form of
Love, a new person .
leaves a mark, remembered as
" Oh we met last October , wish we hadn't "

When ended-
a streak of sadness,
with a sense of dispirit in oneself,
Questioning of my existence-
Hopelessness too.

October and me have had a
Hate- love relationship .But,
It has become a huge part of who i am .
Brings something new to the equation , my life.
October is like an exam for me
How well can you take it?
I am scared but, somewhere I long for October escorted by the festivity

.

5. To joke about him

To joke about him-
"Oh a tortured love poet"
Got to know him,
Grew close .
Understood why he wrote,
What he wrote .
Felt as a personal win.
Never understood someone's
Flaws and accepted it,
So easily .
The only emotion i had ,
was for the imperfections i saw.
Now, I'm the **tortured one**
with crumbled up sheets in my hand
and a hell of a pen.
Carving every glimpse of the one i made fun of.
its everything that i have left .

6. "I love you"

"I love you"
I'm not judging , trust me.
But, whatever you felt-
It's not love my dear .
Its not even liking.
"Just a catch"
That is what it is.
It's love when it's a need
never when it's a greed

You won't expect , just be there-
Witness and not interfere.
Act as the best, for love.
You will suffer .

I'm sure it was not love
I was replaced.
When it's love-
It's just an unoccupied space
If not filled by love
Will forever be it.

7. False percept

I can stand in front of you
Pretend not to even know of you
or you .
I can do what makes you feel unrecognised
Can walk past you without even stealing a glance.
Feel invisible by me-

(I can breathe your presence ,
I choose to be indifferent.
Only if you knew i'm not cold,
You'd think i care-
Not to act as you'd want to perceive.
Find yourself thinking
"Why does she not care?"
In that confusion , i find victory
As you think particularly that
I succeed in my mind ,
even if we lose a loveable interaction , or a connection)

For you, I must remain a false percept .

8. Disapointment

All the thoughts in my head
never delivered on the paper ,
the way i have it in me.
The way it runs around, circles in my mind
but when turned into writing
can never have the same weight.
Can never communicate how i feel exactly
there is still a hint of truth missing

Scrimmages of how i lie to myself.
never upto its potential, just like me.
never conveys my ruminations precisely.

The way it could've been better, like me.
The musings are mine, they are so like me.

A disapointement .
A form of self loathe being re-read.

9. He promised

Very casually,
Definitely in a non-chalant way..
He promised, he'll stay.
At first i didn't believe him.
As my friend ,
It was his duty to make me stop feeling sad.
And in order to do that
He said he'll stay, forever.
He repeated it a number of times.
That is when i felt for him..
Not as a friend but as someone who'll stay forever.
My days were spent thinking about him
And nights talking to him.
Watching him sleep through my computer screen
brought a different kind comfort to me.

The way he lay his head low,
Mouthing the words while he was reading
Mocked me on my silly mistakes
Sounded irritating when he was a friend.
But as a *he promised he'll stay*
Everything changed .

He definitely meant it in a very casual way.
Because he didn't stay.
I mean i will forget him ,maybe?
(His voice echoes every-time some other guy speaks.
He makes everybody not mean anything.)

But the feeling I got
when he assured his presence to me
is still stubborn to stay.
He promised he'll stay.

10. Stars and moon, I can't.

I mean, to bring the stars ,the moon
I can't.
But, i can make you feel important,
If that's enough.
I can get you a necklace with your initial,
only to wear it myself .
I mean i can tell everyone i know,
about how much glory you have .
I mean,
i can tell you the compliments you got from my mother .
I can capture you and reform .
All i can do is try to love you ,
How i'd want myself to be .
It's not the ***comets and constellations*** you want
But it is something .

11. How empty of me, to be so full of you ?

.

How empty i feel , yet so full of you
you aren't really with me .
My consciousness overflows with your memories .
I relive it all back in my head .
Is it worth it being empty to carry you within me ?
A past i still will willingly look back to
Even if its full of flaws painted all over your name.

12. How much of me is already gone?

Whenever i felt like not caring enough
about my absence, The day i'll be gone or dead.
Unalive not present.

When i can't be scared about losing me
-Or even sad ,where i can't feel much about it
I can easily have this thought rest in the back of my mind.

I wonder,

How much of me is already gone ?
How much of me have i already lost?
when i can't mourn my own absence ?

13. Cherished.

-You are so far, unlike everybody I know.

If measured in distance.

But, you got close to me like no one near me could.-

Your words
At night feel like a warm hug to me ,
When I'm shattered,
You hold me tight.

In my head
I urge to give up
And you save me
Every single night,

I feel cherished .

I urge not to live,

you take my broken pieces one by one,

keep them close to you.

You are my comfort, my solace, my solitude

My person,not really -not by any tag .

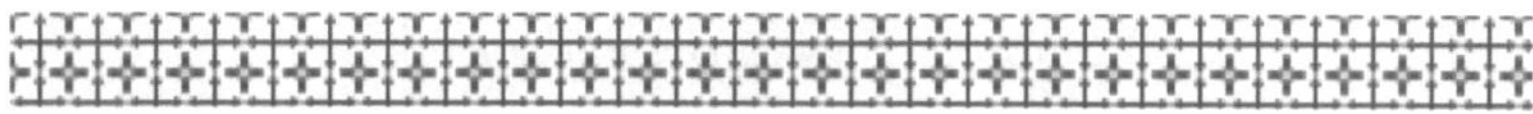

Though ,my nights that I despised ,

makes me want to skip the morning everyday.

Got your hands around me

form your existence on my screen.

14. Understanding/action : A friend .

In my mind, a thought lingers if
a relationship's actual or just left behind.
Understanding's the key, they say.
Searching for a friend to know.
The pain that I feel,
the tears that I've shown.
But people, they can't comprehend.
As time has passed, wisdom took a seat.
I see that everyone understands,
but who's willing to fill the seat?
The seat of the one who takes
action on the pain that I've shared.
The seat of the one who stands up for me,
to merely show they care.
The seat of the one who grasps the reason 'why?'

Everybody understands.
The problem's not understanding,
but showing their friendship will last.

Think about it

Who's willing to take the understanding to their heart?
Who takes responsibility for your pain?
Who truly cares?
• 23 •

When you find someone like that, Love.
Congratulations! You have yourself a friend.

Any other idea you have of a friend
Congratulations again, you've been clowning yourself.

15. Okay,the sidelines it is.

A person, whom i felt enjoyed my company
felt him unconditionally treating me nice
a feeling that maybe he'd be the one
a future bond to look forward to.

"oh ,i will always only love her "
shit, that hurt.
i thought we were starting to get deep ,
even it is as friends.
this time i actually thought someone
could replace the empty in me.
after letting down many,
just because they weren't it.
this paticular one made me slightly slip the thought out .

Well the same story repeats
this time it isn't shocking
i'm the one you only speak nicely too
until you remember the **actual love** of your life
on the sidelines,once again.

16. Space.

Why do you occupy so much space?
Even your absence in my life
echoes volumes about our past.
You couldn't be my possession
leave something to me ,
A fragment something.
I loved the city you reside in before i was even aware of you
definitely adored it more with you
And now every bit of me despises each corner.

I *heard* you're in my town,
<u>Who am i fooling?</u>
Searched for your traces , looked for the sources
You are seeing my city with people you don't like ,
I wish I could've show you it's beauty with my eyes, with me?
Maybe you will reach out or something?
The hell man.
Let me know how to breathe once,
when it doesn't haunt your absence .

Each word of any love song

makes a nerve in me numb

Pains me, your presence in my mind while the tunes,

the lyrics

rest in my head

You haven't let my music be mine too.

Even my writing is you,

i hate my muse?

Let me live , let me forget if not forgive

Hurts enough- you are roaming around my streets ,
ignorant about how it burns my home.

Why burn my house when you don't even care enough to
see the damage done?
Please just leave.

17. ***

The way I was so in love with him,

He never saw it, couldn't grasp the depth.

I'd stay awake ,he drifted off.

I'd watch him breathe through my screen,

Calling his name like he was already mine,

He knew. He always knew.

I loved him in every way he wanted—

If he wanted.

The way I was so deeply in love,

It's like a chain around my heart.

I can't step back, can't let go.

It's like a grip that's too tight,

Holding me prisoner to a past that has slipped away.

The way I was so in love with him,

It's unacceptable, this ache.

Even though he's gone,

Not there for me in the way he was,

I am still here.

It can't be erased.

18. Movies (you)

(read it from your perspective : a general coversation thematic)

its so silly
Romance movies.
beautiful way to spend your time right?...
Dreamy moments, a world that is in front existing in your screen
Its funny that it is made for you but at the
at the very same time it reminds you that it can never be you .
Its so silly..
It's cheery but naive to get caught up in that
How could you be so stupid to even believe that it'd be you
Having a glimpse of the love from the screen,
It can't be you
will never be you

Its so silly..
Of you to think that you deserve the
The airport melodrama,
the angry confessions..or maybe even someone Loving you from a
distance unconditionally

But again..
Its so silly that knowing this truth all along
You'll still get caught up in the sense of belonging
Which leaves you in the spiral of
The love from the screen..and
Arises a question
That will it ever be you?

19. I want me back.

This just isn't me
I don't bleed in paper,
I used to communicate .
Different manner , same feeling
Go back to the time where i expressed
Even if you didn't care , i just did.
Writing to be understood , One time i didn't
Only wrote when asked to .
Now , it's a nightly routine.

I don't even know if I'm writing right?
What is this doubt ?
Am i not good enough to be even expressed in words,
Words that i write myself
how i like, whichever way ?
Is there a format ? i'm supposed to follow.
Or a script?
I don't know, i'm new .
Wish to be more experienced in expressing correctly.

20. Just for once?

The time is ticking away
I still expect you to ring me a bell
Of our memories
Just for once ?
Come back and talk to me the way we did before we grew apart
Just for once?
Laugh repeatedly on the things that weren't funny in the first place
Just for once?
Remind me how you'd never leave my side
Even if it was meant to be a sweet poison
Just for once?

Just for once , I don't want to make ways
for to not remember you, to despise your existence .
Just for once ?
can you make your city look better than mine
- and for me to gladly accept it
No complaints once and for all.

Just for once understand
how *depleting* was it to be in love with you.
Mostly for you to acknowledge
that i was willing to put you above everything .

Or you can just pretend to be mine like you did.
Just for once?

21. Ugly person

How much of an ugly person
I would be
For you to even try to stay and fail
much easier to leave
Hard to love
I wish i knew how..
To be be adored
To be written .
I may hate what i put down on paper
But it stays, trust me
It will remain , to remember.
I won't be, I am not written
Am i making it to hard ?
Definitely it's me .
I'm sorry for expecting.
I forgot I'm me for a second.
Why'd you even try to care-
When I myself don't .

22. FEAR

Oh trust me, it'd be a favour to me to forget you
Forget us, whatever we had.
I wanted to move past it,
the vulnerability i felt.
To skip all the discomfort , the loss of you.
To skip the sulking as a result of your absence .

Now , that i see it finally happening
One way or another
Deep inside me somewhere in the very corner.
I never wanna move past you-
I will lose my idea of love if that happened
As much as i ignore your invasion of my mind ,your thoughts come
creeping in .

As much as i hate it,
i never wanna lose the memory of you,
even if its just to miss you.
The fear of forgetting .

I am ready to bear the nauseating insufferable feeling

of not moving on for the rest of my miserable life .

But i'm still not ready to move past –
Your smile. Your ways .Your opinions .Your effect.

23. The City.

The city, busy in its own realms
seems to pass away swiftly with the time flying.
It catches the pace of the backdrop
I find it usual , never appalling.
I've always compared the city to
scenic beauties of the mountains and the beaches.
The city's rhythm could never catch up to that .
Sitting in the auto where i could see the colours in the sky changing
From blue to yellow to red to
Finally cloaking in dark purple.
No stars in view, makes a starry sky a longing for.
The city has its own appeal, its allure.
Think it when i see the sun at dusk
peeking through the tall skyscrapers.
The city lights at night shine bright,
never let it be dark on the outside, atleast.

The view from my apartment on the 17th floor showcases every little house in sight.

Even the slums lit up with fuzzy lights .

The distances make the lights blur enough to be beautiful in bulk.

Proves how something we made is beautiful.

A late night ride to an isolated cafe,

become a thing for me , hidden gem

a secluded place only i know about

Holds a value to only me and my moments .

I swing between love and disdain for this place.
My affection is inconsistent for it,
just like it's pace.

24. Understand?

I don't mind but I just really wish if you could
Just understand how i love you..
Because I do not know.
Im a self conscious person, but in your words i wanna be lost in
I like to speak more, when its you i want to listen.
The way i want to fall of my bed when you smile.
I like the way you write in your notebook mouthing the words.
I may be jealous;
but seeing you happy in your little accomplishments is the only part
of the day i want to live.
you just being there.
Your this, your that , your girl bestfriend's
even if it's your silly little crushes on my friends.
It is all loveable to me ; shouldn't be
Even the pathetic faces you make on the call.
I just wish you could see how i love you

Don't be in love with me
I just wish you'd understand how I'm so in love with you.
Wish you would know that you make my life liveable.

25. knight in shining armour

A knight in shining armour or..*what a joke*
But I've been left to mend, my heart has grown cold.
No friend in need, no hero true,
Just shattered pieces for show.
I've been broken, since the past did pass,
Left to pick up the shards of my own glass.
No shining armour , no knight in sight,
Just my own two hands, to hold on to myself
Very tight.

I've tried to find some feeling, in the eyes of others,
But they've all departed, like autumn's leaves .
I've come to realize, that even the best,
can leave me forever broken.

I need a knight, with a heart of gold,
I need a friend, to stand by my side,
But I'm not sure, if they'll stay, or let me slide.
For even if I find one, who's strong and true,
An actual knight in shining armour
They'll still leave me broken, like the rest did too.

So I'll keep on searching, for a *real hero*
Once again,having being caught myself in this loop again
But until then, I'll just have to heal.
The wound within, is one that won'tbe better ,
Until I find a friend, who'll truly bemy solace.
For now I'll just hold on, to the pieces of my heart..
And hope that someday, I will also find a knight to start.

26. Everything that is me In this moment has a hint of you, just a little bit .

(Poet's pov)

Everything that is me In this moment
has a hint of you, just a little bit .
But enough for them to see that you left a mark,
more like a scar .
All my words and mentions circle back to you .
My mind races to clues related to you.

I talk about your city like it's the most
beautiful place in the world.
It was just a city before,
that i had visited several times.
Then i got to know you lived there.
I got excited by the fact that i have been
to places where you have spent your whole life .

I could only notice its eternal beauty
when it came from your words .

Glad that it happened

Sad that i won't be able to appreciate it anymore.

The words no longer can be heard.

A simple cologne or maybe a sweet desert

that I don't even like.

stays in my mind like no other information i ever seeked.

PLAYLIST

Hurt by now?

Nothing's New - Rio Romeo

Silver Soul - Beach House

Good Luck , Babe! - Chappell Roan

Beautiful Boy - Esha Tewari

Iris - The Goo Goo Dolls

Look After You - The Fray

loml - Taylor Swift

Fade into you - Mazzy Star

Rosyln - Bon Iver , St. Vincent

27. Just good enough?

(poet's pov- a personal favourite . It's how i see me.)

Just good enough.
If there was a perfect phrase to describe me
It would be "just good enough"
let me give you an idea of "just good enough"
This should be able to explain.
just good enough to catch your eye,
just for a moment,not very long.
not good enough to be kept there as a vision for your future .
we are just starting to get at it
starting to get to the fact that
i'm just good enough to play a part,
never to be the lead
just good enough to be there for your help.
After that, always left trashed .

Just good enough
to be the girl you'll find cute or pretty for a while ;
not good enough
for you to find me beautiful no matter what i do,
or how hard i try.
just good enough-
to be the girl whom you will always love second.
just good enough
to be your someone, not "the one" .
just good enough
to fit in with you.

Just good enough be your option, an option which'll never
turn to your choice .
Because i'm "just good enough" to exist.
if you know what i mean.

28. Better to preach

There is a click i get
Whenever you hate me
I preach this brutality.
Despise me. Loathe me .
Curse my name , be cruel.
Remember me in ways you don't want to .
Try to forget me and fail.
Plot against me
Play all odds .
For that i'll thank

Let your hate be its purest form
If not love , i'll sustain in hate.
Even better .
As hate can can never be pretence
Love can and have been pretence,
all my years.

29. Until

well , i can't force one to read , can i ? but i really hope in some way or another it gets to the person it belonged to :/

I used to judge people
For how they feel after a breakup
The pain , the urge
I used to judge them as weak and shallow
For putting their emotions above their self respect .
I used to judge them for feeling
alienated towards their particular someone,
For being too dependent on others.

I used to hate people who felt like
they lost their world because of losing
that one person.
Because How can it be that deep?

I had this notion until **i lost him.**
We never "broke up"
That wasn't needed .
But some lines that are once crossed
can't be set back again.

I haven't stopped judging "weak people".
I just added one more name to the list of people i hate for such behaviour.
Mine.
Well ,for all i know..it was pretty much ; very deep.
I didn't know what losing my world feels like
Until i lost you.

30. Birthday to me .

26/07 3:08 AM

Wishes and virtual kisses
matters a lot to me
Heartfelt affirmations from a bunch,
attention and the short-lived love.
The act of being important,even for a day.
It's nice even if it's just for
the sake of one pitiful day
I wait every year for it ,
always thought that no one could change
the particular feeling of being valued ,
At least this once.
Then i talked to you on the call
You wished me happy birthday
As if its a burden you have ,
As of that moment ,
i became a charity case .

for me all wishes came down
to the worth of absolutely nothing.
But trust me ,

I was there for your charity case ' of a wish.

i'm addicted to this certain kind of sadness.

Ignoring all my bazzilion
'I value you' wishes , I only wanted yours.
I got your sympathetic one.
One poisoned seed ruins the whole harvest.
I never thought that this day would be
ruined, just like that- in one phone call.
You took my sense of 'being valued' once and for all
Tossed it in front ,with a cloak of " i do care".

I dont feel loved now
all feels like a burden.
Happy birthday to me.

31. I hate me .

I hate me.
I'm tired with the pretence of me
being the main character of my life
but i am not
I hate humans
The most? Me.
I do not care about me.
I wish i'd die right at the spot
if only it was in me
I have such great presence,
for show.
I wish i had some self esteem to end this.
I don't vision a future
Nor will i-
The world would actually be better off
One less unlovable shit of a person
Self- aware yet no betterment, what use ?

I wish someone else would hate me to the extent i do myself

.

• 53 •

If they did
They'd kill me
And that is a favour i want.

32. Empty.

I feel...
Not much, just a void
That tells me—
"I'm sorry, Aanya. You have nothing to care about."
There's no point in trying;
Why even bother?
This feeling might seem ordinary,
But it's the first thought that hits me,
The one that makes me question.
It's the thought that says,
"Why do you keep trying to think or feel?"

This emptiness isn't just normal;
It's a deep empty space
A pull that makes life seem like a cruel joke,
Where fading away feels like the only escape.
It's the root thought,
The quiet voice that drowns out everything else,
Leaving only deep, dark emptiness.

33. Oh Stranger

Stranger,

don't enter in my life to fix what's broken.

Trust me.

you did succeed .

You made it survive ,

the shattered lifeless one in me.

But after the fixation

please don't break the same joints ruthlessly that you helped fix ,

even worse.

Now ,

they are aren't mendable,beyond that.

And as of now , you aren't a stranger,

even if i want you to be .

Not anymore.

34. *

He really isn't there anymore
Its 12 AM and i'm reminiscing .
How i used to pen down his comments and laughter in my silly little
verses.
Started off as a journal of happiness
Turned into a need of an unloved soul
But, today he isn't here.
I let him go, i was bleeding
I lost my everything
In order to save something
i had to let him go
He was never mine
But now,
He just isn't there anymore
And it hurts like a bitch.
What hurts even more that I can't say that
I hate him , i don't .
can't say that all i'm left with is a broken friendship
'Cause you weren't just a friend.

35. Stage.

A person Who was never scared of

Public speaking spaces and stages

Comfortable with hundreds of people ; fumbled on the stage

For the first time i had a brief encounter of what i've had nonexistent

for years ,

Nervousness .

All the self esteem built over all those years, dropped to zero ,took

barely ten seconds .

A hundred wins could never make up

For that one loss .

The eyes on me which didn't matter

Felt like they were judging me

Standing became harder

I could feel the shaking afterwards

The disappointment of messing it up .

Stayed of days, weeks and months.

Although it recovered ,

It was a one time thing

But before being on the stage

That fear creeps in

I make it through the show ,barely
i bury my nails in hands
Not allowing it to shake
My trembling voice is covered with the act.
But god that feeling
Always creeps in.
I hope i never fumble again,or else
How will i be on stage?
It was the only other place i felt comfortable on.
Felt like i belonged to there.
How will i ever be comfortable in the place which taught me how to
live in my own flesh?
I must not fumble, can't afford it.

36. Feeling deep

They say feeling deeply is a *boon*
Every feeling gets heart to head
Your heart skips a beat for a simple missed call
The highs of life make you want to scream
A simple flirt makes blood
rush into your cheeks,
for all to see.
I feel, and all i have felt lately is
anxiousness and disappointment deeply .

The blushing is cute though ,
But ,

Nobody ever talks about the heart shattering

where it paces to process the demolition .

The itchy feeling in the chest
when the pain is so unbearable
It makes you wonder
Why still continue to breathe?
Even the tiniest comments,
Stains your personality

painting what you do or don't.
Feeling deeply is a curse.

<u>*(leaving space for you to express what feeling deeply means to you express the writer in you)*</u>

37. Unlovable. Unrequited. Undone.

I'm what you might have a notion of
Unlovable
What is there to cherish?
I'm the definition of what you call
Unrequited, all my life, unresolved.
Just like an **undone** knot ,

Every time i try to assemble into
Being capable of something real.
I remember that i'm someone you call conceited , vain.
"she deserves what comes to her"
Living under the cloak of the shallow perception of being confident.
For you to not see the real me.
Because i'm not vain in my mind space.

I cry ,
my head buried in the pillow
Until i can't catch my breath
Until I'm not comfortable in my own skin ,
Can still feel it burn.
I hide my swollen eyes just enough for you not to notice ,
to believe i'm cold.
it has made me weak in my bones
What i really am is
Fake, Unlovable and condescending.

38. Phases.

Falling out (i)

I'm slowly falling out of love,
Never thought it was possible with you
But all of a sudden
You cross my mind rarely and i don't feel the surge of heavy loss
I feel acceptance. I might be completely over it
If given more time
It was harsh, but now it's happening
Its good to know that i won't hold you back .
But it would've been so nice
If you could've just been mine
I never would have to do this, go through all of this .
This is one of the rare times that I think about you
When the clock has struck midnight and no one's around
Sooner or later i will forget you and your face
Sadly, your calming voice too.
You'll now be alive in my midnight scrimmages
Of how i loved and fell out of love with you.

Nope , i was wrong . (ii)

Could never
My soul could never.
A minor inconvenience and he flooded back in
He mapped my life , got used to it
Got into a fight with my mother
And all i could remember is his words

"oh she wishes the best for you just like i do ,my love."

It'd never be the same
A hole in my life, his absence
It will truly remain my greatest loss, for eternity .
Nope, i was wrong,
couldn't possibly fall out .

39. Father's Daughter

Father and daughter, dad and his little princess

Not so little anymore , was never the princess type was i?

well i think it has its pros and cons

We aren't normal.

Neither you are a normal father

nor am i a normal daughter

We push ourselves to a limit which is unbearable for other people but

bearable for us,

Barely for me .

Well talking about any other relationship

Having a wife, a brother , a close colleague

A father -daughter relationship takes a huge turn , It is chaotic.

Mentoring a girl

while trying to understand her situation must be hard.

But i was an easy child.

You weren't able to do it formost.

I'm pretty unstable , i'm sorry.

You are trying to , i bet.

So ,

we have our ups and downs

There are many times that i have let you down and many times you
have let me down.

But saying that is wrong or bad is just baseless, don't want to complain
like every other relationship

It has life .

*it is like a roller coaster..and roller coasters are scary but
fun aren't they..?*

I tell myself this , to feel convinced

For you to pay attention,

to appreciate me

For once , i have forgiven.

I am not the perfect child you deserved

maybe settle for the imperfectly perfect?

You might not be cheery at my best times

but you were there consoling me at my very worst.

I am a person who believes money can get everything

I can never return this favour in money.

I just wish we were more through.

40. Weigh

It doesn't weigh on his heart like it does on mine.

I spoke to him today—
Casually, normally,
In his words these would be the words
Casual or normal. While every word for me is heavy,
monument of some meaning
Knowing what he is to me.

And it doesn't even faze him.
I shatter daily, Wondering
"What should I have done differently?"
There he is,
Still chatting, still casual.
As if it's all a game to him.
Call me selfish;
but i'd want him to feel what i do .
Even if its for someone else.
But if it weighed on him,
If it really pressed on his soul, like it does on mine.
Casual wouldn't be in his vocabulary.

41. **

You came in time

Changed the course of the story

i didn't want to be a part of in the first place.

You made me like my story.

You made me believe it was worth living

Being naive, i did.

I had lost all my main characters

all alone .

You,my precious person , you.

I can never thank you enough for being there every single time

You stopped making me regret every bad decision

Until you were the very 'Bad decision' i needed.

For a while, i got whatever i lost back

Something even better

That is you , my precious, my heart.

When it comes to writing about you

I don't mind being the poet when my muse is you.

I'd rather pen you down in my heart than existing as a piece of poetry

myself.

I'd rather prefer not having all of you to even have a negligible

something

I can't afford to lose you now

It makes my tears urge out which haven't reached my cheeks from a

time I can't recall

You out of all people make me feel

Make me feel rage,anger,envy and out of all the things you make me

feel

The one i seem to hate is

fear

Fear of loving you so much .

You won't be there at one point of time .

I'd lose my everything again.

None of me will matter,

If there's no you, my present would not be explained.

42. Incapable to be in love againn

I used up all my heart and being to be in love with you
Now, i'm incapable of falling in love ever again,
If it's not you.
It's not like i can't try,
I just don't want to .

You hold the highest pedestal in my mind.
You aren't replaceable.
No one can fill that space

Every other i talk to , i start comparing .

Every face is a reminder,
A trace of how i will never not be in love with you.
And no one could ever compete to that

At least in my mind.
And just like that i'm back to square one
Incapable of falling in love ever again.
Because if not you ,then it better be no one .

43. Wish i didn't care

I'd rather not pen you down with tears in my eyes
slowly slipping from my cheeks
I wish I didn't have to write this just to contain myself,
all because of how you are.
oh, i just wish i didn't care
wish i didn't bear .
I bear with the pain of you
you taking a step in my vain
polishing my decisions with your name .
Oh ,i wish i didn't care.
I wish I could **not** care how you react to my actions.
My feelings get interrupted by your presence
it leaves no room for me to breathe
i feel suffocated ever since you mattered .
All i breath is your presence and your ways .
You consume me,
and i wish i didn't care .

Didn't care enough to even hate you for how you are ,

to accept we aren't meant together .

44. I am the words i write

Cliché it may be,
but its deeply how i feel.
I am the words i pen down on a saturday night .
Came to my notice that there is a world
completely out of my sight ,in my mind
in the words i write.
The thoughts i crumble upon ,
moments i stifle-
a quarell or an eventful day in my mind
all being relived by certain people,mostly me.
Reveries that stay on the cusp of my tongue
the events that i elude from-
contained briefly in the words i write.

vivid visions of my existence,that i hate
coded for anyone to get me,
an open letter to you all , know me-
maybe you wouldn't despise me the way i do-
they you'd know i'm no better than them or you
i'm worse, as i'm aware.
read through me, the guilt is whispering
through the words i write .

love me or loathe me
you will only truly know me
when you interpret the words i write
-the way i hate myself.

I hate them for making me write
only if i could say it,
wouldn't have to have these words written all over me
perhaps then i'd be something more than the words i
write.

45. Funny

Its relentlessly funny to me
that exchanging some words can lead to
a beautiful friendship,
blind and uncanny it may be-

could never see the faults in the bond then
clear as day when i see them now
still retains its beauty somehow

some whispers turn into confiding in the other
finding excuses to see each other
seeking fun and solace in the very company

the person isn't a friend anymore
he or she becomes a habit
a habit I couldn't get rid of on my own
but it eventually gets rid of me.
I lie there , still an *addict*

their presence remains ,
written all over

a memory that will never not stay

influences my take on the world
i always have them in my subconcious
forcing me to view things their way
the essence of their short-lived presence.

46. Easy Child .

It wasn't a choice, role of the easy child.
Wasn't easy either.
A child , must be filled with innocence embodied,
Never let a child be the "**mature one**" too early as -

After a period of time,
the exhaustion takes over them.
They just weren't meant to bear at the time.
All the maturity sinks into something that doesn't seem to matter
anymore.
Perhaps to now drown in bunch of unclassed emotions.

The imaginary weight of being the *"easy child "*
the necessity to perform , inability to accept failure
to be upto one's potential ,always.
to be everything all at once,
to never bother the other and compromise,
to just never mess up ,We aren't allowed to,

No, we didn't break things at people's houses.
Instead shatter inside everyday carrying the same baggage
to a different extent of being an easy child
even after growing up
oh i wish , i never had to be that
i wish i'd just simply be , let me free.

47. Embrace the race

Have you ever felt the shiver ?
anxiety whispers "you aren't doing right by yourself"
In a place where you don't belong
Heart feels out of place,
questioning every step you take.

"Why am i here, what is the point of this race, will it leave me benefited or just with a scarred joker face?"

"Will it result in me being successful?"

"Will i be left behind?"

The feeling of not choosing correct.
The feeling you get of having a chain
of constraints around yourself
which ensures you can't have a clean slate,
The path feels uncertain,unclear
Leaves in deep chaos and thought

Well, burdened by thoughts don't lose your way
Your path will find you if its not either way
In the heart of the journey, embrace the race.

48. Connected to you

(This is the worst one i have with me . But it is the first i ever wrote , i was scared to express then . It was the best i could do at the time. Well, it's the last and the least . But it was a start , so i respect it . Here is the unedited version .)

You still creep in my mind,invade

I hate it i really do..

You don't affect me now

neither do I miss you or something

But that one particular word

of even a quote that you used

which I used to cherish is now unbearable..

I despise it.

I despise how your memories still creep in my mind.

invade my space like you own it.

You really don't

It's not that I love you anymore. I really don't

But God I really once did.

I won't deny it

The difference is

You were in my prayers and I was in your countable "aquaintances"

Every memory ,Every single lyric is torture .

i hate it when you still matter

Invade my space

And make me despise

Every lyric

Every note
Connected to you.

Letters.

A letter i just couldn't send(1)

God i hate you so much.

Yes,i hate how i love you

I hate that i love all of you

All that you have and that does include your

Your unsolicited annoying opinions.

    I say "stop bothering me "

I want you to blabber all you have in mind .

I hate how i enjoy every single word with or without meaning from you

"Stop this stupidity " i say,

While i value every kind of opinion

Take it into consideration and ponder.

    "Leave me alone, i don't wanna talk to you"

    While i wait for you to come back with a cunning smile and talk to me
like nothing happened

When it did.With all the new judgements for me .

    God, i love being mean to you

And What i love even more is how you take crushing words like a beautiful
flower bouquet

cherish them with your usual cranky smile.

"Never talk to me "

"Why are you doing this to me "

Well that is true .I do not know what you are doing to me

Or whatyou want with me .

But yet again every other day i hear your laugh ,

mocking me ,

Criticising me

Showing me what that kind of love feels like

Im not sure if its love

But it feels nice

Nice to know someone who is existing

no motive ,just staying

Mine ? you aren't.

what is the harm to think you are

Because i don't see you going anywhere.

Yet , I hate you

For not saying anything to me

I wish you would .

I wish you could .

But God,

i just hate how my will to wake up everyday is your words

that i pretend to hate,

not able to have a goodnight sleep without.

A letter that I just couldn't send (2)

"it's okay now , but did i deserve it ?"

i say this to others , for you i have this

why the hell did you do this to me ?

No , i can't be friends with you

not anymore.

you were my life, my sun and my glory

i travelled to another god damn city for you

just to catch a glipse

couldn't even face you after covering 300 miles

acted like i didn't wanna see you ?

because i knew you wouldn't give in .

why did you say you loved me?

why did you have to start that ?

why did you ask those deep questions about me ?

why'd you stay the whole night ?

why did you sleep on the call everyday just to make me comfortable?

why'd you made me feel like the best person in the world?

why'd you remember everything i let out of my mouth ?

why'd you remind me i was special?

No friends do not do that . K?

I fell in love.

Don't you blame me again , you already have .

No it wasn't a joke ,when i lost you .

i haven't been feeling anything other than your absence.

You say i pushed you away,

which isn't a lie, i did .

It killed me enough to wanting to be with you .

But the fact that i wanted you to stop me,

to convince me for once to stay,

for you to even put up a pretence of care.

why'd you let me go , did i not matter ?

am i that worthless to you?

that shallow?

It hurts , that it didn't hurt you just as much.

its selfish i know.

I can never love someone now .

i haven't cried for someone in so much pain.

You didn't have to lie

could've just said

"No, you did not matter ".

You didn't even reach out once , man .

Even as a friend, you owed me atleast that .

My chest , it physically pains now

I hate your name , the city, the blueberry cheescake.

This prose, because you were the writer i was the reader

welcome to this shitshow,

You are my muse .

For me you will be the one i lost , a misery , a strong regret

you'll never know , even if you do-

you'll never care would you?

because when i told you , i was never acknowledged

only blamed.

Anyway to explain others clenching my heart i say

"Its okay, but did i deserve it?".

LETTERS.

Here's Your Abrupt Ending .

"Mom i really wanna 'be someone'"

"Darling you already are someone "

" No, you don't understand ,not like that..
In the world's eyes...in their mind."

" Darling, the success you show to the world can be fabricated, if you really want to have the feeling of 'being someone'. This must be your first step."

"what?"

"Stop believing that you will be someone when someone tells you are. -"